Gogol's Coat

CARY FAGAN • ILLUSTRATED BY REGOLO RICCI

Tundra Books

Published in Canada by Tundra Books, *McClelland & Stewart Young Readers*,
481 University Avenue, Toronto, Ontario M5G 2E9

Published in the United States by Tundra Books of Northern New York,
P.O. Box 1030, Plattsburgh, New York 12901

Library of Congress Catalog Number: 98-60386

Canadian Cataloguing in Publication Data

Fagan, Cary
    Gogol's coat

ISBN 0-88776-429-0

I. Ricci, Regolo.   II. Title.

PS8561.A375G62 1998   jC813'.54   C98-930680-1
PZ7. F33Go 1998

We acknowledge the support of the Canada Council for the Arts for our publishing program.

We acknowledge the financial support of the Government of Canada through the Book
Publishing Industry Development Program for our publishing activities.

Design by K.T. Njo

Printed and bound in Canada

1 2 3 4 5 6   06 02 01 00 99 98

For Rachel and Sophie, with love

C. F.

————

To Victoria

R. R.

*I*n an old city, on the third floor of a dreary building, at the end of a dim hallway, was a room. A sign on the door of the room read: OFFICE OF ALPHABET COPIERS, THIRD CLASS, and inside the room stood rows of desks and chairs. On each of the chairs sat a man or a woman whose job it was to copy out the alphabet from *A* to *Z*, in neat large letters, without missing a single one, or getting the order wrong.

And what was done with these alphabets? They were posted in classrooms all over the country so that girls and boys could learn to read.

But at one desk sat not a man nor a woman, but a boy. His name was Gogol. Gogol was the best alphabet copier of all.

Gogol was a serious boy with red hair, curly and unkempt. He was so much smaller than the others that he had to sit on a fat book to reach the top of his desk.

But he was the most industrious of all the employees of the OFFICE OF ALPHABET COPIERS, THIRD CLASS, and never stared idly out the window, or doodled funny faces when he ought to be working. He also had the most elegant handwriting.

And Gogol loved his work. He was happy only when copying out letters, his tongue wedged in the corner of his mouth. Particular letters were favorites with him: he always grew excited when he had to draw a *B* or an *H* or a *W*. Smiling, he sometimes whispered their names under his breath.

Among the other employees was an exceedingly jealous man named Ravinsky. Gogol's beautiful alphabets made his work look hurried and smudged in comparison. Ravinsky was a stout man, who considered himself a dandy and wore a waistcoat and gloves even when he worked. Sometimes he would jog Gogol's hand as he passed by, ruining a letter. Once he tossed bits of paper over Gogol's head and asked the boy when he was going to get married. Another time he stuck a note reading PINCH ME onto Gogol's back, so that all day people gave him pinches on the arms and legs.

One day when work was finished, Gogol put on his tattered overcoat and began to walk home. The gas lights were already lit, and the warm breath of horses pulling wagons could be seen in the chilly air. When Gogol looked at people, he thought they resembled letters – a plump man looked like an *O*, a skinny woman like an *I*, a bent over apple seller like an *F*. He crossed the Emperor Bridge and hurried through streets and alleys.

*H*ome was a small room with a very small window. Gogol warmed up a bowl of cabbage soup to eat with a bit of bread for his supper. Just when the soup was ready, a small dog leapt onto the outside windowsill, pushed the window open with her nose, and jumped down into the room.

The dog was a stray. On her first visits, she had been afraid of Gogol, but he had slowly won her friendship, naming her Rose because the marking on her fur resembled the letter *R*. Now he shared his dinner with Rose and sent her out again, as the landlady did not permit dogs in the house.

Afterwards, Gogol went straight to bed. He wanted to be well rested for the next day's work. As always, he dreamed of the letters of the alphabet – letters with animal faces, letters that played musical instruments.

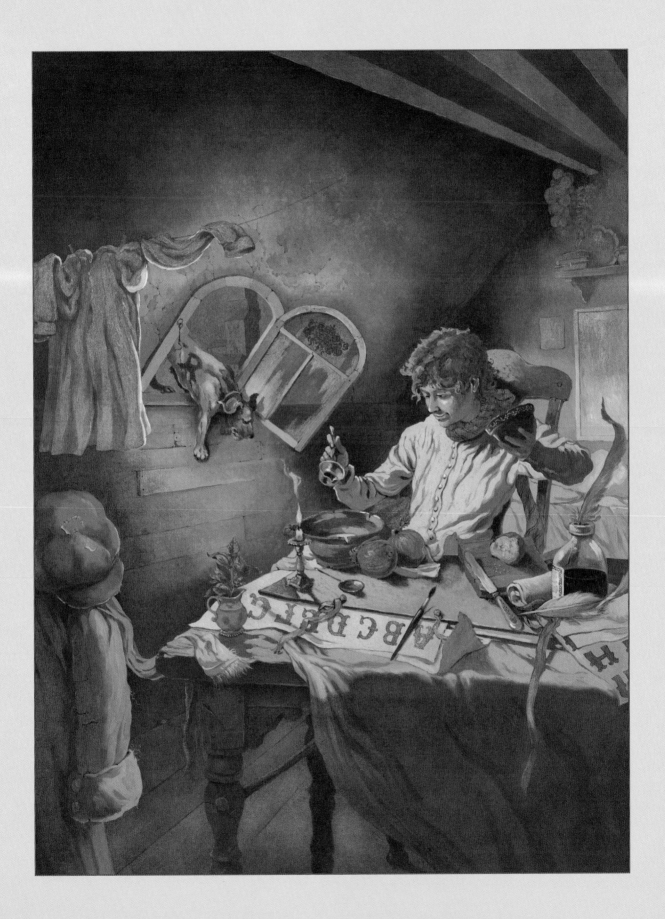

Rose was a smart dog, and Gogol had taught her to wake him up in the morning. She came in through the window, barked twice, and then gently grasped the top of the quilt with her teeth and pulled it down to the end of the bed.

This morning his teeth chattered. The wind blew into the room and, when Gogol got up to close the window, he saw that winter had arrived. Snow covered the roofs, the railings, made white hats on the tops of the lampposts. More snow was falling.

Quickly Gogol dressed, made porridge for them both, and pulled on his overcoat. By the clock in the tower he could see that it was almost time for work. With each step he grew colder and colder. His overcoat was worn so thin that the wind whistled through it. On the shoulders and elbows were patches, and on the patches were more patches.

When he arrived at the OFFICE OF ALPHABET COPIERS, THIRD CLASS, the other employees saw him shivering. "No wonder you're as cold as a statue," Ravinsky said with a laugh. "There isn't enough coat there to wash behind your ears!"

Gogol tried to warm himself at the stove before starting to work. But his hands remained so chilled that his *A*s came out weak instead of firm, his *W*s droopy instead of bouncy. The whole alphabet looked like it was ashamed of itself.

Rose waited for Gogol in the office doorway and, when work was over, they walked together down the street, Gogol with his shoulders hunched against the cold. Smoke drifted up from the chimneys, and the shop windows were etched with frost. Gogol knew that he couldn't go through the whole winter like this, so instead of going straight home, he headed for the lodgings of Levick the tailor.

Levick lived in an attic at the top of a dark and winding staircase. Trousers, jackets, and shirts in need of repair hung from the ceiling. He was a sour-faced man who grunted more than he spoke, but he was famous for being able to mend clothing that other tailors had given up as hopeless.

When Gogol and Rose arrived, the tailor's wife was making dinner, and the attic smelled of fish stew. Levick himself sat on a large table with his legs crossed and with bare feet, sewing the seam of a dinner jacket. The end of a pin stuck out at the corner of his mouth, and lengths of thread hung around his neck.

"You rascal of a needle!" Levick cried. "Don't want to be threaded, eh? We'll see who is the master and who is the servant."

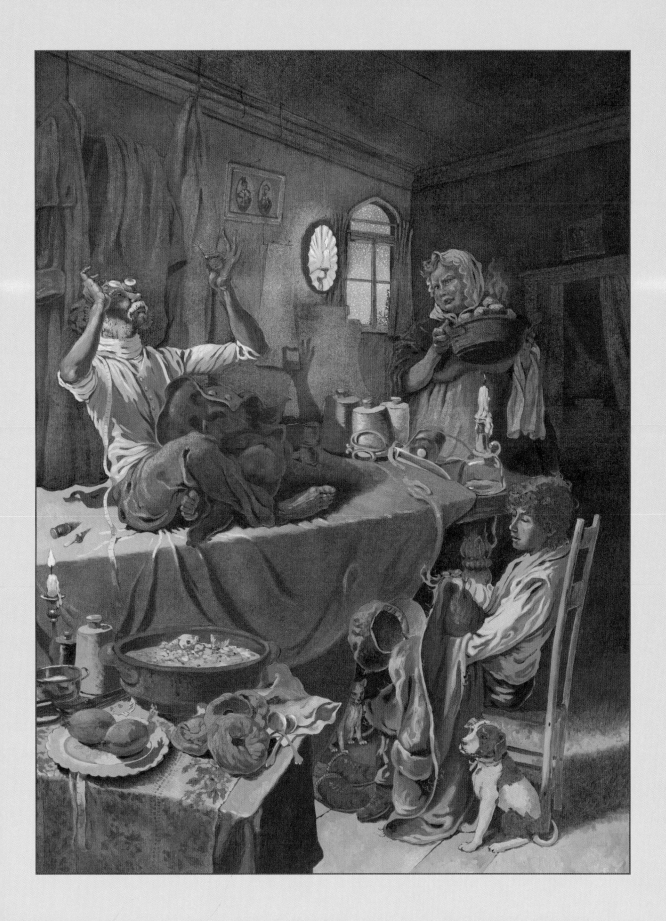

Gogol took off his overcoat to show it to Levick. "It's a little worn, I admit," Gogol said, "but perhaps a few new patches and some stitches in the lining . . ."

Levick snatched the coat from Gogol's hands. "I'll be the judge of what's needed." He held the coat out and shook it so vigorously that Gogol feared it would fall to pieces. "Impossible," the tailor pronounced. "I'll have to make you a brand new overcoat, that's all."

Gogol's heart sank. A new coat was bound to be expensive. Every week he managed to save just a little money, so that now, after many months, he had ten silver coins, which he kept in a stocking under his bed. He asked the tailor, "Can you make me a nice coat for ten silver coins?"

"Believe me, you won't want to take it off – that's how nice it will be."

Gogol swallowed. "All right," he said. "Make me a new coat."

A new coat! Gogol felt as if his life had suddenly become important and special. The tailor ran the measuring tape around Gogol's waist, under his arms, across his back. Then they went to the shops looking for cloth. Levick dismissed one as too loosely woven, another as too coarse. Finally he found a cloth that was heavy yet fine, sure to keep out the wind. They bought silk to line the inside of the coat and to make it soft as a caress.

*L*evick worked on the coat for two long weeks. He used the finest thread and sewed double seams for extra strength. Knowing Gogol's fondness for the alphabet, he cut a letter G – Gogol's initial – out of red velvet and sewed it onto the lining.

Every day that Gogol waited, the winter became more harsh. It was so cold at night that he couldn't even dream. The city was sheathed in ice. Even the hands of the clock in the tower had frozen.

One morning Rose came in to wake him up, but Gogol could hardly bear to get out of bed. A knock sounded on the door. "Come in," Gogol said through his blue lips. In stepped Levick the tailor with the new coat over his arm.

"It's finished?" Gogol asked.

"To the last stitch. And if I do say so myself, it is a masterpiece."

Gogol sprang out of bed and got dressed. The tailor held out the coat for him to slip on. What a fit! It fell so perfectly on Gogol's shoulders that it felt almost like his own skin. How substantial and yet light! How soft the inside! How warm! Tears of joy came to Gogol's eyes.

"My customers are always satisfied," Levick said with a smile.

*H*ow happy Gogol was as he walked to work! The city was gripped by the most terrible winter anyone could remember, yet he felt warm and snug in his new coat. People looked at him admiringly as they hurried by. Rose barked with pleasure, as if to announce his coming.

The news spread quickly at the OFFICE OF ALPHABET COPIERS, THIRD CLASS. "What a magnificent coat!" they cried, slapping him on the back. Even Ravinsky came over and felt the sleeve. "A coat like that is too good for the likes of you," he muttered.

After work the other employees insisted on taking Gogol to a restaurant to celebrate his possession of such a coat. They held up their glasses and made long speeches. Someone recited a poem; another performed the trick of pulling handkerchiefs out of Gogol's ears and doves from his coat pockets. They ate herring and drank many glasses of tea. The restaurant orchestra played waltzes and mazurkas, and one of the women insisted that Gogol dance with her.

All the attention started to go to his head. Gogol began bragging about the quality of the material, the rich silk of the lining, the double seams. "Ten silver coins I spent – my entire savings!" he told them. "But it was worth it. Nobody has a coat as fine as this one."

When the party broke up, it was almost midnight. The horses were sleeping in their stalls; the shops had closed their shutters; even the night watchman was dozing. Gogol began to walk home, warm in his coat, his boots making new prints in the snow. Rose walked sleepily at his heels.

They came to the Emperor Bridge. Gogol noticed a few dark figures lingering halfway across. As he and Rose passed by, one of the figures called out, "Hey, that's my coat you've got!"

"No, it's mine," Gogol said. But before he could run, strong hands took hold of the collar and began to yank it from his shoulders. Gogol tried to resist; Rose growled and snapped; but in a moment the coat was off and the dark figures were running away.

His coat was gone – stolen!

W hat could Gogol do but brush the snow from his trousers and walk home in the cold? The next morning he had to go to work in his old, tattered coat. All day and for the rest of the week, he worked without pleasure, each letter feeling like a heavy burden.

The wind blew yet more cruelly, and the old coat was no defence against it. The chill that Gogol felt during the day would not disappear at night, and he shivered miserably in bed. Rose too suffered from the cold and, even though the landlady didn't allow it, he let the dog stay in his room during the night. The two slept side by side, sharing each other's meager warmth.

One morning Gogol dragged himself to work. On the steps of the office building, he saw Ravinsky entertaining the other employees of the OFFICE OF ALPHABET COPIERS, THIRD CLASS, with jokes and wisecracks.

"Hey," Ravinsky sneered, looking disdainfully at Gogol's tattered coat. "Here comes a raggedy scarecrow. Don't you know there aren't any wheat fields to guard around here?"

Everybody laughed. But Rose raised her tail in the air and began to growl, as if to tell Gogol something. And then Gogol realized what. Ravinsky was wearing his new coat! It didn't fit him exactly, for it was short in the sleeves and the buttons were straining with the size of Ravinsky's belly.

"You're the one who stole my coat!" Gogol cried.

"I don't know what you're talking about," Ravinsky said. "I had this coat specially made. And I must say, it's keeping me as warm as a steaming samovar. If you think this coat belongs to you, then you'll have to prove it."

"Just open it up," Gogol said. "There's a red *G* inside – that's my initial."

"If you insist," Ravinsky said with a gleam in his eye. He opened the coat, but instead of the *G* there was only a patch of brown cloth sewn onto the lining.

"Satisfied?" Ravinsky said.

Gogol despaired. He knew that the coat was his, but how could he prove it? And then he had an idea. He knelt down beside Rose and, as he stroked her head, he whispered into her ear.

"That mutt should be on a leash," Ravinsky said uneasily.

Rose barked twice and crept up to Ravinsky. And just as if she were pulling the quilt off Gogol's bed in the morning, she grasped the top of the patch with her teeth and started to pull.

The patch was not sewn with a double seam, nor was the thread knotted properly. In fact, it was a poor job altogether and, as Rose pulled, the thread began to unravel and the patch to come away in Rose's teeth.

There underneath was the red velvet *G*!

"Why, that *is* Gogol's coat," the other employees said with amazement. They took the coat from Ravinsky's shoulders and gave it back to Gogol. Gogol removed his old coat, tossed it towards Ravinsky, and put on the new one.

Ravinsky ran down the street and over the Emperor Bridge, the tails of the tattered coat flapping behind him, until he could be seen no more.

After that day Gogol was never cold. He wore his beautiful new coat all winter, and on the coldest days he picked up Rose, tucked her inside the coat, and carried her along. At bedtime he draped the coat over the bed to keep them both warm and snug.

And every night he dreamed of his beloved letters, falling like snowflakes over the city.

AUTHOR'S NOTE

More than 150 years ago, a writer named Nikolai Gogol lived in Russia.
This Gogol wrote a story for adults, called "The Overcoat," about a man
whose new coat is stolen by thieves. Alas, he never gets it back.

"The Overcoat" has become one of the most famous short stories
ever written. When I first read it, I felt very sorry for this poor man
and for a long time I used to imagine how the ending might have been
different. And so I have written this story, about a boy named Gogol,
in order to have the coat returned to its rightful owner.